WHAT DOES THE Tooth Fairy DO WITH OUR Teeth?

By Denise Barry

Illustrated by Andy Boerger

To the loves of my life:
Ray, Samantha, Nolan and Louie Barry.

To my friend and fellow author, Mason Winfield,
for his insight and inspiration.

To my dad, Ray Ventola,
and my sisters, Dawn and Renee.

In loving memory of Mom and Darlene.

~Denise Barry

To Junko and Mika.

To the two Roses in my life,
my mother Rose and Rosie the Ferret.

And to M.M., my own personal "tooth fairy."

~Andy Boerger

www.mascotbooks.com

For more information, please contact:
Mascot Books
560 Herndon Parkway #120
Herndon, VA 20170

info@mascotbooks.com

Library of Congress Control Number: 2014940893

CPSIA Code: PRT0716B
ISBN-13: 978-1-62086-841-6

2nd Edition

Printed in the United States

WHAT DOES THE Tooth Fairy DO WITH OUR Teeth?

WRITTEN BY
Denise Barry

ILLUSTRATED BY
Andy Boerger

The Tooth Fairy flies to the house on the hill
and peeks at a boy from his windowsill.
"Look at that treasure," she says out loud.
"Such a clean, shiny tooth. That makes me so proud!"

She'll stop by again when he's sound asleep
and pick up his tooth without making a peep.
What will she leave him? Some money? A toy?
Whatever it is, he'll be one happy boy!

Why does the Tooth Fairy fly here and there
collecting teeth from children everywhere?
She must have a ton, a million, or more!
But what in the world does she use them for?
With your head on your pillow
and tooth underneath,
let's imagine what the Tooth Fairy
does with our teeth!

Does she put each tooth in a little glass case
and tie a bow around it with a red shoelace?

Does she dust them with a feather
each and every day,
just in case her friends stop by
to check out her display?

Maybe she cooks them all up in a pot
and throws in some cotton, in just the right spot.

12

Out comes a cloud as big as a jet.
Down comes the rain, getting Fairy all wet!

13

Does she make one long necklace
to share with her friends
to wear to the Moon Dance
all fairies attend?

While they danced in the dark
would it swing to and fro?
How their faces would shine
from its dazzling glow!

15

Maybe those teeth make a mountain so high
she climbs to the top and shakes hands with the sky.
And if that hill crumbles, the Fairy will fall.
But since she can fly, there's no worry at all!

Could the Tooth Fairy's house
have a secret room?
A shop filled with magic
and each afternoon,
she works on the teeth
she collected at night
and turns them to presents
she knows are just right.

Have you noticed the sparkles inside of the snow?
How do they get there? Does the Tooth Fairy know?

Does she scatter our teeth through the snow way up high?
Then change them to glitter as they fall from the sky?

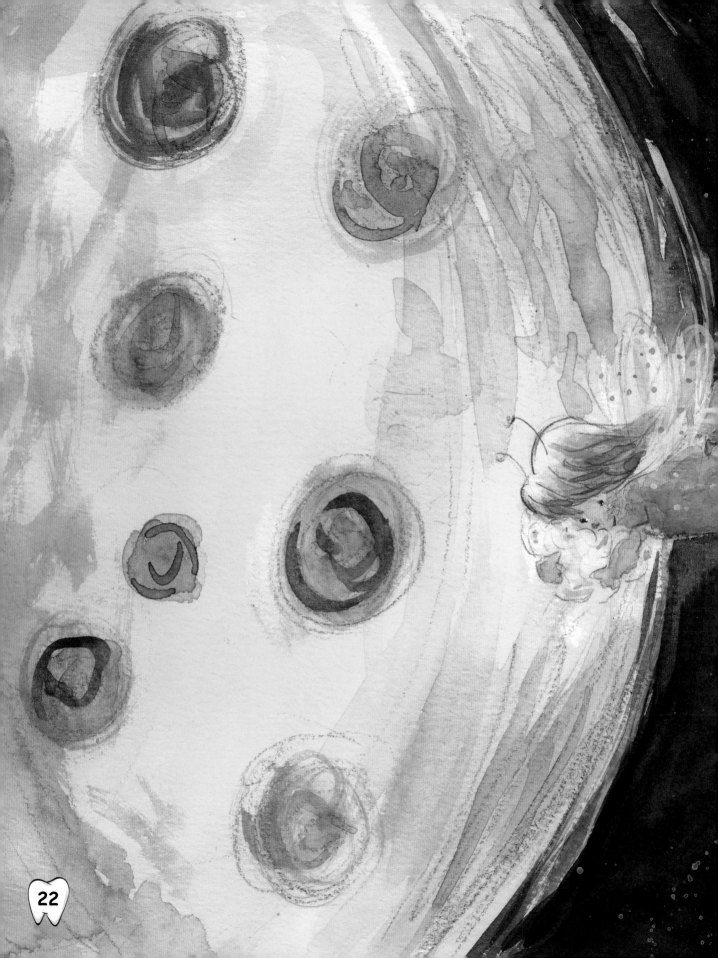

How close to the moon does the Tooth Fairy soar
with her arms so full she can hold no more?
Could the tiny bright stars that hang in the sky
be the teeth that fell down as she flew by?

Where does the Tooth Fairy live, do you think?
And does her front yard have a skating rink?
Did she fill up a circle with teeth on her lawn
and make something only a fairy skates on?

Sometimes it's stormy flying over the seas.
If the Tooth Fairy drops a few teeth in the breeze,

would they fall to the waves and get lost in the swirls?
Would they land inside oysters and turn into pearls?

When the Tooth Fairy's tired from flying so far
does she stop for a rest on top of a star?
Does she toss some teeth to the man on the moon?
Does the moon want to play, or should she leave soon?

What if she's hungry and wants a sweet snack?
Can she take a few teeth from out of her sack?
And with just a touch of her wee fingertips
turn them into cookies with chocolate chips?

Does she drop a few teeth on the sandy shore
to turn into scallops and oysters and more?
Would your parents believe you're telling the truth
if you say your seashell had once been a tooth?

Now it's your turn to think of a brand new way
the Tooth Fairy might use your teeth one day.
What will she do next? Hey wait, could it be?
What if the Tooth Fairy is really a he?

34

Do you have an idea for what the Tooth Fairy might do with our teeth? I want to hear it!

Enter it in my **Tooth Fairytale Contest** and you could win a prize.

Go to denisebarry.net/tooth-fairytale-contest to enter and check out all the **Fairy Fun Stuff** while you're there too.

Fairy good luck!
Denise Barry

P.S. You're never too little to dream big, nor too big to dream!

Denise Barry is the award winning author of the children's picture books, *What Does the Tooth Fairy Do with Our Teeth?* and *Soap On A Rope.* She is also an inspirational writer whose work has been featured on various websites and in the best selling book, *Watch Her Thrive; Stories of Hope, Courage and Strength.*

Denise is currently working on a middle grade book called *Sweeney Mack and the Slurp and Burp Competition,* so watch for that! Also, check out her Raisin' Kids blog—for parents who want to raise children who become adults, not adult children. Go to denisebarry.net.